Rumpelstiltskin

Mara Alperin

Illustrated by
Loretta Schauer

NAME GAMES

SNEAKY SPELLS

Learn to Spin

LITTLE TIGER PRESS
London

There was once a foolish miller, whose pride and joy was his beautiful daughter, Isabel. She was sweet and gentle, and adored by all.

To Grandma Nina, who told me this story on the way home from Pullen Park ~ M A

For Ariane xx ~ L S

LITTLE
TIGER PRESS
1 The Coda Centre,
189 Munster Road,
London SW6 6AW
www.littletiger.co.uk

First published in Great Britain 2014

Text by Mara Alperin
Text copyright © Little Tiger Press 2014
Illustrations copyright © Loretta Schauer 2014
Loretta Schauer has asserted her right to be
identified as the illustrator of this work
under the Copyright, Designs and Patents Act, 1988
A CIP catalogue record for this book is
available from the British Library

ISBN 978-1-84895-709-1
Printed in China
LTP/1400/1010/1214
2 4 6 8 10 9 7 5 3

The miller was so proud of Isabel that he boasted about her, day after day, to **anyone** who would listen . . .

"Tulips start to bloom when my daughter sings," bragged the miller.

"When Isabel catches raindrops, they turn into butterflies."

"My daughter can even spin straw into gold!"

Soon word reached the king, who rode to
the village to hear the miller's amazing tales.
"Gold from straw?" the king cried,
greedily. "How clever! I command you
to spin for me tonight!"

"Wait!
There's been a terrible
mistake!" shouted Isabel. But it
was too late – and she was
carried off to the castle.

There, in the highest tower, was a small, wooden spinning wheel ... and a mountain of straw.

"Spin me my gold!" ordered the king. "Or I shall throw you into the royal dungeons."

Poor Isabel tried everything she could think of ...

She pedalled the wheel, and she twisted the straw ...

She pushed and she pulled ... but nothing worked.

And as the stars began to twinkle, Isabel started to cry.

"If only there was someone who could help me!" she wept.

Suddenly, there was a **dazzling** flash of light, and **POOF!** a strange little man appeared. He had a sharp, pointy face, and a glittering **golden** cape. "I can **spin** straw into **gold**," the little man smirked. "And I will help you … for a **price!**"

"But I'm just the miller's daughter," whispered Isabel. "I have nothing to give."

"Here's my plan," he said. "Tonight, I will spin your gold. But one day, when you have riches beyond your dreams, I shall return. You **must promise** me my pick of treasure then."

"Yes, anything!" Isabel agreed, gratefully.

So the little man sat down
at the wheel. **Whirrrr! Whirrrr!**
Around it spun, making coins,
and crowns,

and trinkets,
and trophies...until the
room glittered with gold.

"You saved me!"
sighed Isabel. "How
will I ever repay you?"

"Just don't forget your
promise," laughed
the little man.
And with that,
he vanished.

In the morning, the king returned. He was
delighted! "What glorious gold!"
he cheered. "You truly are a wonderful girl.
You must come and live in my castle –
I'd like you to meet my son,
Prince Herbert!"

Unlike his father, Prince Herbert was handsome and kind. He and Isabel fell in love at once.

Soon wedding bells rang out across the land!

The years passed and the happy couple were blessed with a beautiful baby boy, Prince Hugo. They were so happy, in fact, that Isabel forgot all about the funny little man …

Until, one stormy night, as the lightning flashed,

POOF!

the little man appeared **again**.
"It's **me**, my pretty one!"
he cackled. "I'm here for the
treasure you
promised!"

"What treasure would you like?" Isabel asked. "Gold? Silver? A diamond necklace?"

"No!" sneered the little man. "I want something even more precious. I want…"

" ...HIM!"

And he pointed right at Hugo.

"No!" cried Isabel in horror. "You can't take my darling baby!"

"Very well," the little man purred. "Then how about a game? If you can guess my name before three nights have passed, you can keep your baby."

And chuckling, the little man leaped into the air - and vanished.

"Don't worry, my love!" called Herbert, rushing over. "That horrid man will never take dear, sweet Hugo."

On the **first** night,
Isabel guessed all the
names she'd ever heard.

Nick? Ned?
Norbert? Willy?
Wally? Weatherby?

"No, no, NO!"
giggled the little man.
"That's not my name!"

The **second** night, Isabel and
Herbert were up until dawn,
thinking up new names.
"Is it ... Bumbleknuckle?
Grubblegrunt?
Wiggleboo?"

"No, no, NO!" cheered the little man. "Not even close!"

Isabel was desperate. "I can't think of any more names!" she cried.

"Then we must find out this little man's secret," said Herbert. "I have a plan..."

So, the next morning, Herbert
set out to search for the little man.

He rode through
the village . . .

Then, as the sun was setting in the woods,
he saw the flash of a golden cape. Herbert hid
behind a tree, and watched as the little man
danced around a fire, singing . . .

over the hills,
and deep into the forest . . .

But the little man
was nowhere to be found.

"The Queen will never win this game,
Rumpelstiltskin is my name!"

"That's it!" Herbert whispered.
And he rushed back to tell Isabel.

That night, the little man appeared one final time.

"This is your last chance, my pretty one!"

"Let me think," said Isabel. She frowned and scratched her head. "Could it be...

Rumpelstiltskin?"

"Doom and darkness! How did you guess?" shrieked Rumpelstiltskin.

And he howled and he growled, and he stomped,

and he stamped...

So hard that he crashed right through the floor and fell down,

down,

down,

deep into the royal dungeons below.

Rumpelstiltskin was never seen in the kingdom ever again. Hugo grew up to be gentle and kind, and adored by all – just like his mother.

And so they all lived
happily ever after.

My First Fairy Tales

are familiar, fun and friendly stories – with a marvellously modern twist!

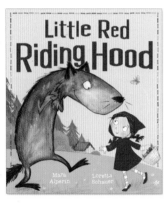

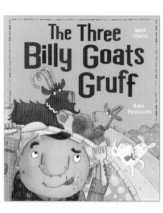

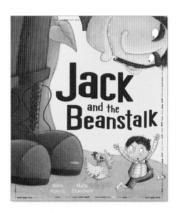

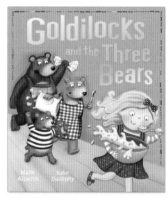

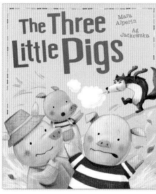

Pssst! coming soon!

The Elves and the Shoemaker

The Ugly Duckling